PUSHKA

by *Stephen Mackey*

Hodder
Children's
Books

A division of Hachette Children's Books

THE
CIRCUS
IS
COMING!

It's puffing into the magic wood
every wagon full of clowns
and laughter.

Except that in the last wagon, Pushka is fast asleep in his bed. Little does he know that he is about to topple out...

…amongst the enchanted trees. He wakes in fright.
Where is he? And what's that noise?

THUD
THUD
THUD!

It sounds like ENORMOUS footsteps, getting nearer and nearer.
Scared, Pushka runs away through the night until he spies…

…the most beautiful girl, dancing alone under the stars.

She says not a word, but she beckons him to her.
Then she whirls and twirls in his arms, as light as thistledown.

Oh, Pushka! Lovely Lulu is in the power of
a cruel giant who wants to eat you for supper.
In his hands, she is only a little puppet on strings.

'Starlight and moonshine, my heart is in danger
As I look into the eyes of a handsome stranger,' sings Lulu, sadly.

The magic of her song flows over Pushka like a wave.

Even the birds and animals
are in her spell.

Bewitched and bedazzled, Pushka follows as Lulu leads him to her house. Has she prepared a delicious feast? Strawberry pie and sugar cakes?

But what's this? A little door in the trees?
Oh, Pushka, take care! You're in deepest danger!

Lulu is opening the little door.
Pushka peeps inside and CRASH!
The door swings shut and he's trapped inside the giant's oven!

The giant smiles and
hangs up his beautiful
puppet in a tree, sure
that she can't escape.
But a stronger power
than his is at work.

Lulu's little wooden heart is full of love for Pushka and she's not afraid of her master any longer.

Magic flutters through
the air like falling leaves
as she begins a new song:
'Mice dear, you clever things,
Nibble away these cruel strings.'

The little mice gnaw through the puppet's strings. Lulu can move by herself, just like a real girl. She is free!

But what of poor Pushka,
alone and trapped
in the evil giant's oven?
Red hot flame rises into
the darkness and the water
spray from his button hole
does no good at all. He is ready
to give up in despair.

But look!
The oven door is
opening and Lulu,
burning with love,
has come to
save him!

They scramble out of the oven just as the hungry giant arrives
to make supper. His yell of fury shakes the kitchen as
he finds that Pushka's gone.

Faster and faster! Pushka and Lulu
run down the twisty, turning
pathways until they see their
way to freedom.

But in the magic wood, even the paths are enchanted
to trap the runaways.
Giant feet are stamping up behind them and a giant voice shrieks:
'I'll get you! Oh, yes, I will!'

Lulu desperately begins
another magic song:

'Birds of the air!
My love and I
need your help if
we are to fly!'

And the birds carry them
gently down the mountain.

Not a moment to spare! For the cruel giant is hollering:

'Fee-Fie-Foe-Fum,

I'm coming to get you if I can!'

But he can't reach them – yet.

Pushka and Lulu wander this way and that, tired and hopelessly lost amongst the enchanted trees.

All of a sudden,
a light glimmers
through the branches.
Has the giant found
them, after all?

"I'll never leave you!" cries Pushka, as whatever-it-is comes closer and closer.

It's the circus! It's come back to rescue little Pushka!

'I was lost until I found you,' says Pushka, as they jump into
the last wagon which is empty, waiting for them.
'But together we can do anything.'

And together in the circus, they enchant
children all over the world with the magic
of their singing and dancing,
their laughter and happiness.

The End

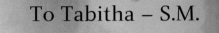

To Tabitha – S.M.

First published in 2011 by Hodder Children's Books
Copyright © Stephen Mackey 2011

www.stephenmackey.com

Hodder Children's Books, 338 Euston Road, London, NW1 3BH
Hodder Children's Books Australia, Level 17/207 Kent Street, Sydney, NSW 2000

The right of Stephen Mackey to be identified as the author and illustrator of this Work
has been asserted by him in accordance with the Copyright, Designs and Patents Act 1988.

A catalogue record of this book is available from the British Library.

ISBN: 978 1 444 90134 4

Hodder Children's Books is a division of Hachette Children's Books
An Hachette UK Company
www. hachette.co.uk